Sara at the Store

The Sound of S

by Cecilia Minden and Joanne Meier • illustrated by Bob Ostrom

The Child's World®

Published by The Child's World®
1980 Lookout Drive
Mankato, MN 56003-1705
800-599-READ
www.childsworld.com

The Child's World®: Mary Berendes, Publishing Director
The Design Lab: Design and page production

Library of Congress Cataloging-in-Publication Data
Minden, Cecilia.
  Sara at the store : the sound of S / by Cecilia Minden
and Joanne Meier ; illustrated by Bob Ostrom.
    p. cm.
  ISBN 978-1-60253-416-2 (library bound : alk. paper)
  1. English language—Consonants—Juvenile literature.
  2. English language—Phonetics—Juvenile literature.
  3. Reading—Phonetic method—Juvenile literature.
  I. Meier, Joanne D. II. Ostrom, Bob. III. Title.
  PE1159.M573 2010
  [E]—dc22   2010005607

Printed in the United States of America in Mankato, MN.
July 2010
F11538

NOTE TO PARENTS AND EDUCATORS:

The Child's World® has created this series with the goal of exposing children to engaging stories and illustrations that assist in phonics development. The books in the series will help children learn the relationships between the letters of written language and the individual sounds of spoken language. This contact helps children learn to use these relationships to read and write words.

The books in this series follow a similar format. An introductory page, to be read by an adult, introduces the child to the phonics feature, or sound, that will be highlighted in the book. Read this page to the child, stressing the phonic feature. Help the student learn how to form the sound with her mouth. The story and engaging illustrations follow the introduction. At the end of the story, word lists categorize the feature words into their phonic elements.

Each book in this series has been carefully written to meet specific readability requirements. Close attention has been paid to elements such as word count, sentence length, and vocabulary. Readability formulas measure the ease with which the text can be read and understood. Each book in this series has been analyzed using the Spache readability formula.

Reading research suggests that systematic phonics instruction can greatly improve students' word recognition, spelling, and comprehension skills. This series assists in the teaching of phonics by providing students with important opportunities to apply their knowledge of phonics as they read words, sentences, and text.

This is the letter s.

In this book, you will read words that have the **s** sound as in: *store, sandals, sack,* and *silver.*

Sara likes to go to the store.
Today, Mother needs
new sandals.

They walk down the street.

There is Mr. Summers's store.

"Do you sell sandals?"
says Mother.

"Yes," says Mr. Summers.
Mother buys some sandals.

Sara sees a sign.

BIG SALE TODAY

Let's buy some surprises!

Sara sees some sugar candy.

Her brother, Sam, likes candy.

They buy him a sack of candy.

Sara sees a bag of seeds. Dad needs seeds for the garden. They buy Dad some seeds.

Sara sees a sewing basket. Nana likes to sew. They buy Nana a sewing basket.

"Let's buy you a surprise, too, Sara. What would you like?" says Mother.

Sara sees a silver ring.

"That is the surprise for me!

Thanks, Mom!" says Sara.

Fun Facts

Do you have a pair of sandals? They are probably made from leather, rubber, plastic, or cloth. The oldest pair of sandals dates back 4,000 years. The shoes came from Egypt and were made from papyrus, a reed that still grows in Egypt. The oldest sandals in this country date back 2,000 years and came from the Anasazi Indians. These sandals were also made from reeds. Sandals not only protect your feet from harmful things, but they also help keep your feet cooler in hot weather.

In ancient times, silver was often used to make coins. Today, however, Mexico is the only country where silver coins are used as a form of everyday money. But silver continues to have a variety of uses. When you eat dinner, you might notice that your fork and knife are made of silver. Perhaps your mother owns some silver jewelry. Look around your home. You might see silver candlesticks and a silver candy dish.

Activity

Making Silver Play Money
Gather some cardboard, tinfoil, nickels, dimes, and quarters. Trace the outlines of these different coins on the cardboard, and have an adult help you cut along the tracing. Next, cover the cardboard circles with tinfoil. You can't use this money at any real stores, but it's perfect for playtime at home!

To Learn More

Books
About the Sound of S
Moncure, Jane Belk. *My "s" Sound Box®*. Mankato, MN: The Child's World, 2009.

About Sandals
Bradman, Tony, and Philippe Dupasquier (illustrator). *The Sandal*. New York: Viking Kestrel, 1990.

Hickox, Rebecca, and Will Hillenbrand (illustrator). *The Golden Sandal: A Middle Eastern Cinderella*. New York: Holiday House, 1998.

About Silver
Baumgartner, Barbara, and Amanda Hall (illustrator). *All My Shining Silver*. New York: Dorling Kindersley, 2000.

San Souci, Robert D., and Yoriko Ito (illustrator). *The Silver Charm*. New York: Doubleday Books for Young Readers, 2002.

Sterling, Kristin. *Silver and Gold Everywhere*. Minneapolis, MN: Lerner Publications Company, 2010.

Web Sites
Visit our home page for lots of links about the Sound of S:

childsworld.com/links

Note to Parents, Teachers, and Librarians: We routinely check our Web links to make sure they're safe, active sites—so encourage your readers to check them out!

S Feature Words

Proper Names

Sam

Sara

Summers

Feature Words in Initial Position

sack

sale

sandal

say

seed

sell

sew

sewing

sign

silver

some

sugar

surprise

Feature Words with Blends

stick

store

street

About the Authors

Cecilia Minden, PhD, is the former director of the Language and Literacy Program at the Harvard Graduate School of Education. She is now a reading consultant for school and library publications. She earned her PhD in reading education from the University of Virginia. Cecilia and her husband, Dave Cupp, live outside Chapel Hill, North Carolina. They enjoy sharing their love of reading with their grandchildren, Chelsea and Qadir.

Joanne Meier, PhD, has worked as an elementary school teacher, university professor, and researcher. She earned her BA in early childhood education from the University of South Carolina, and her MEd and PhD in education from the University of Virginia. She currently works as a literacy consultant for schools and private organizations. Joanne lives in Virginia with her husband Eric, daughters Kella and Erin, two cats, and a gerbil.

About the Illustrator

Bob Ostrom has been illustrating children's books for nearly twenty years. A graduate of the New England School of Art & Design at Suffolk University, Bob has worked for such companies as Disney, Nickelodeon, and Cartoon Network. He lives in North Carolina with his wife Melissa and three children, Will, Charlie, and Mae.